SUPERJOE DOES NOT DO CUDDLES

Michael Catchpool

Emma Proctor

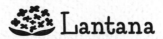 Lantana

SuperJoe was up and ready to go. He had a busy day ahead of him.
It's not easy being a superhero, you know.

His mum was ready as well: ready to give him a great
big cuddle before he went out.

"Superheroes **don't** do cuddles!" said SuperJoe. "What
were you thinking? I've got people to save. There's
a terrifying tiger on the loose!"

"Well, you're not going out without your scarf," said Mum.
"You'll catch a nasty chill."

SuperJoe was not impressed.

"What use is a scarf to a superhero, especially when you're catching ferocious tigers?"

But Mum wouldn't take no for an answer... so he had to wear it.

Off went SuperJoe to save some anxious tourists who had just had an unexpected encounter with a very hungry tiger.

"My superhero senses tell me that my arch-enemy the Grey Shadow has been making mischief," said SuperJoe. "That tiger didn't get here on its own!"

SuperJoe didn't mess about — superheroes don't. He dealt with the tiger
just like that and led it back to the wild where it belonged...

...and was home in time for tea.

SuperJoe had no time to waste. He was
needed urgently. "I'm off!" he said.

"Not before you've had a cuddle with your mum!"

"Superheroes **don't** do cuddles!" said SuperJoe.
"I've got a runaway train to deal with! The engine's
going one way and the carriages the other."

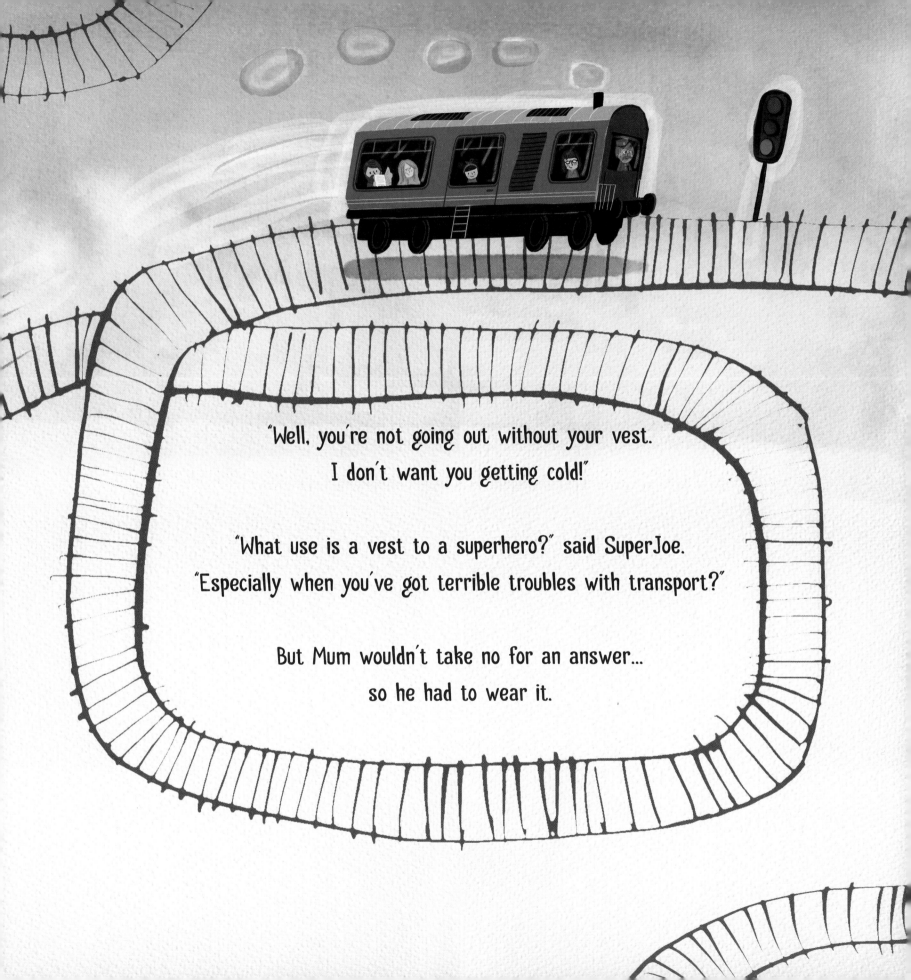

"Well, you're not going out without your vest.
I don't want you getting cold!"

"What use is a vest to a superhero?" said SuperJoe.
"Especially when you've got terrible troubles with transport?"

But Mum wouldn't take no for an answer...
so he had to wear it.

SuperJoe shot off — as only a superhero can. "Call it super-intuition, but I think my evil nemesis the Grey Shadow has something to do with this," said SuperJoe.

And then he set about sorting out the runaway train and getting things back on track.

SuperJoe was so efficient, he even got the train to the station five minutes before it was actually due...

...and was home in time
for a long, hot soak
in the bath.

SuperJoe was raring to go — there was an emergency.
Emergencies are what superheroes do best.

"Don't forget a cuddle before you go," said Mum.

"If I've told you once, I've told you a thousand times:
superheroes **don't** do cuddles. Not even one!"

"Well you're not going out like that — just look at those pants!"

"They're not my pants, they're my superhero shorts!"

"They look like pants to me," said Mum. "You need a belt to keep them up."

"What use is a belt when you've got to save people from a collapsing bridge, over a raging river, deep in the jungle?"

But Mum wouldn't take no for an answer...so he had to wear it.

"I spot the wicked hand of my foe the Grey Shadow at work here! Bridges over raging rivers in deep, dark jungles don't go collapsing on their own, you know."

SuperJoe set about a super-rescue...and he didn't even stop to sign autographs.

And though there were a lot of people to save...

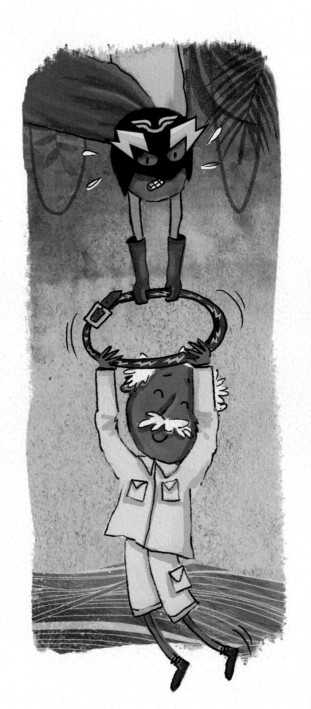

...he made it back in time for bed.

"There have been far too many perilous predicaments and dangerous goings on recently. I really want to give someone a piece of my mind!" said SuperJoe.

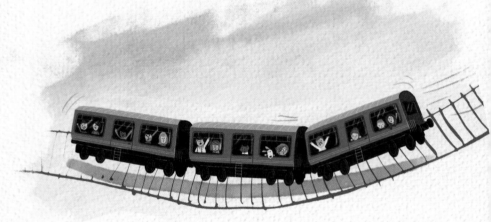

"Not tonight, you won't," said Mum.
"It's bedtime."

And she turned off the light.

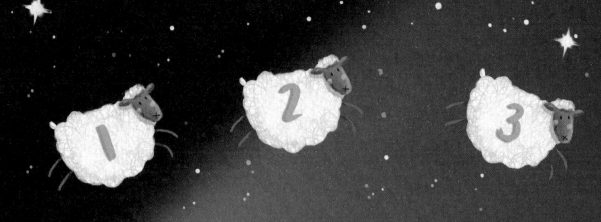

But SuperJoe couldn't sleep.
He lay all alone in the dark, turning this way and that.

Until Mum came in.

"You need a warm, milky drink — that always helps."

"Superheroes don't do warm, milky drinks," said SuperJoe.

"Well, what about a song?"

"No silly lullabies or counting sheep or anything like that!"

"Then what do you need?" asked Mum.

"Just one thing." And SuperJoe whispered in Mum's ear.

"But... I thought superheroes definitely didn't do..."

"Ssshh," said SuperJoe quietly, "don't tell everyone!

I mean, what would the Grey Shadow say?"